T0065968

# B IS FOR BOY

# GOD OF WAR

# B IS FOR BOY

WRITTEN BY ANDREA ROBINSON

ORIGINAL ILLUSTRATIONS BY ROMINA TEMPEST

INSIGHT EDITIONS

San Rafael • Los Angeles • London

AND SO, WE ARE ALONE NOW, JUST US TWO.
*NO*, I AM NOT AFRAID OF SPENDING TIME WITH MY SON. ARE YOU?

WE WILL USE THIS TIME FOR LESSONS.
LIKE A IS FOR AXE, STEADFAST AND TRUE.
AND B IS FOR BOW, WHICH YOUR MOTHER MADE FOR YOU.
AND B IS FOR BOY, WHICH MEANS YOU.
IT'S GOING TO BE A LONG TRIP.

C IS FOR COME, BOY. CONTROL YOUR ANGER, CLOSE YOUR HEART.
AND DO NOT TOUCH THAT FALLEN TROLL;
WE KNOW NOT WHERE IT HAS BEEN, FOR A START.
THAT'S WHAT YOU GET!

D IS FOR DARK, LIKE THE JOURNEY AHEAD . . .
WAIT! DO NOT JUST RUN OFF. YOU WILL END UP IN TROUBLE—OR DEAD.
WHOA!

E IS FOR **ENERGY,** YOURS IS MUCH GREATER THAN MINE.
WE WILL PLAY THE QUIET GAME, UNTIL WE REACH THE NEXT SHRINE.

F IS FOR FREE WITH OUR BUSINESS, WHICH YOU CERTAINLY ARE.
DO NOT TELL THIS WOMAN IN A TURTLE I HATE PEOPLE—THAT IS GOING TOO FAR.
WELL, YOU DO.

AND WHO IS SHE TO SAY I SHOULD TELL YOU I AM A G, AS IN GOD?
I DO NOT NEED ADVICE FOR MY OWN SON!
GODS ARE BASTARDS, GODS ARE $%&*(), GODS ARE—
. . . IT IS NOT IMPORTANT, MOVING ON.

H IS FOR **HER,** THE MEMORY BETWEEN US.
DO NOT MISTAKE MY SILENCE FOR LACK OF GRIEF—
IT IS NOT SOMETHING I WISH TO DISCUSS.

I IS FOR **IT WILL SERVE YOU TO STOP TALKING.**
NO, YOU CANNOT CARRY THE ASHES, BOY. KEEP WALKING.

FOR J IS FOR JOURNEY, BY NOW OURS HAS SURELY LASTED YEARS
. . . YOU SAY IT IS NOT EVEN HALF OVER? SOMEHOW, THAT IS NOT HOW IT FEELS.
WE'RE GOING TO JÖTUNHEIM, RIGHT?

K IS FOR **KNIFE.** DO NOT LOSE IT AGAIN.
THIS IS ALL YOU GET—THEY DO NOT GROW ON MOUNTAINS.

NOR DOES L IS FOR LEVIATHAN, COMMISSIONED BY YOUR MOTHER.
I TAKE CARE OF MY AXE, BY GIVING IT TO THIS HACK AND HIS BROTHER.
I WILL MAKE IMPROVEMENTS TO THE AXE.
BUT NOBODY ASKED YOU TO.

**M** IS FOR **MIMIR,** SMARTEST MAN BROUGHT LOW.
THIS SATYR IS FULL OF UNWANTED ADVICE AS WELL—WHAT DOES HE KNOW?

N IS FOR NO. NO, WE WILL NOT GO ON THIS FOOL'S QUEST, WE WILL NOT GATHER BONES. ARE YOU LISTENING, BOY? . . . FINE. NEXT TIME I MEAN IT, THOUGH.
WHY ARE THESE BONES ALL OVER THE PLACE?

O IS FOR **ODIN,** ANOTHER PETTY GOD AND HIS MEDDLING PROGENY.
I BLAME A CYCLE OF BAD PARENTING WHEN IT COMES TO MAGNI AND MODI.

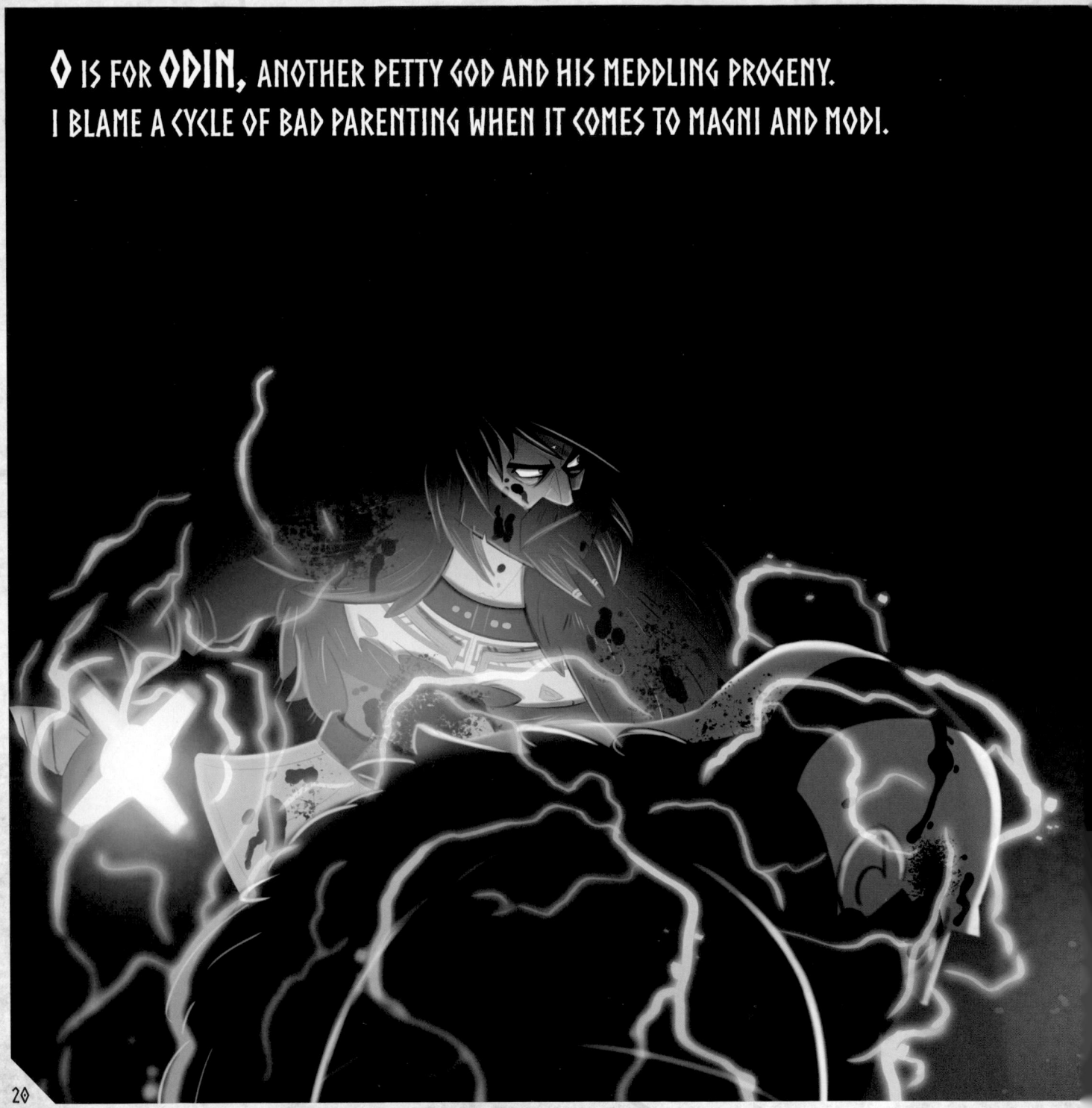

STOP IT!

P IS FOR PROTECT YOU—FROM ENEMIES, FROM MY PAST.
BECAUSE THE THINGS I LEFT OUT ARE TOO DARK, TOO VAST.

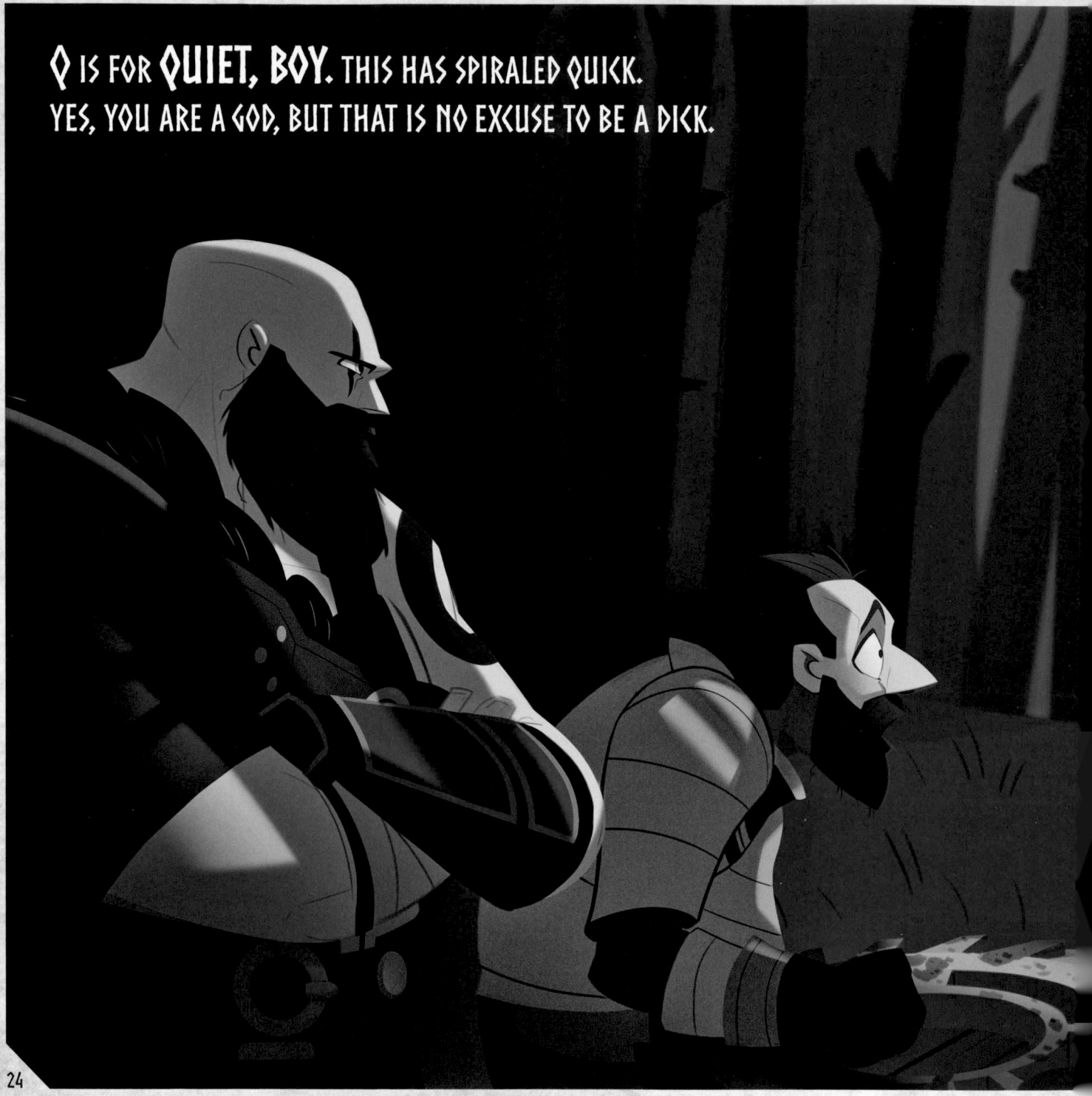
Q IS FOR QUIET, BOY. THIS HAS SPIRALED QUICK.
YES, YOU ARE A GOD, BUT THAT IS NO EXCUSE TO BE A DICK.

R IS FOR **RESPONSIBILITY,** OVER WEAPONS AND MIND.
YOU ARE POWERFUL, BUT WE MUST BE BETTER THAN ALL HUMANKIND.

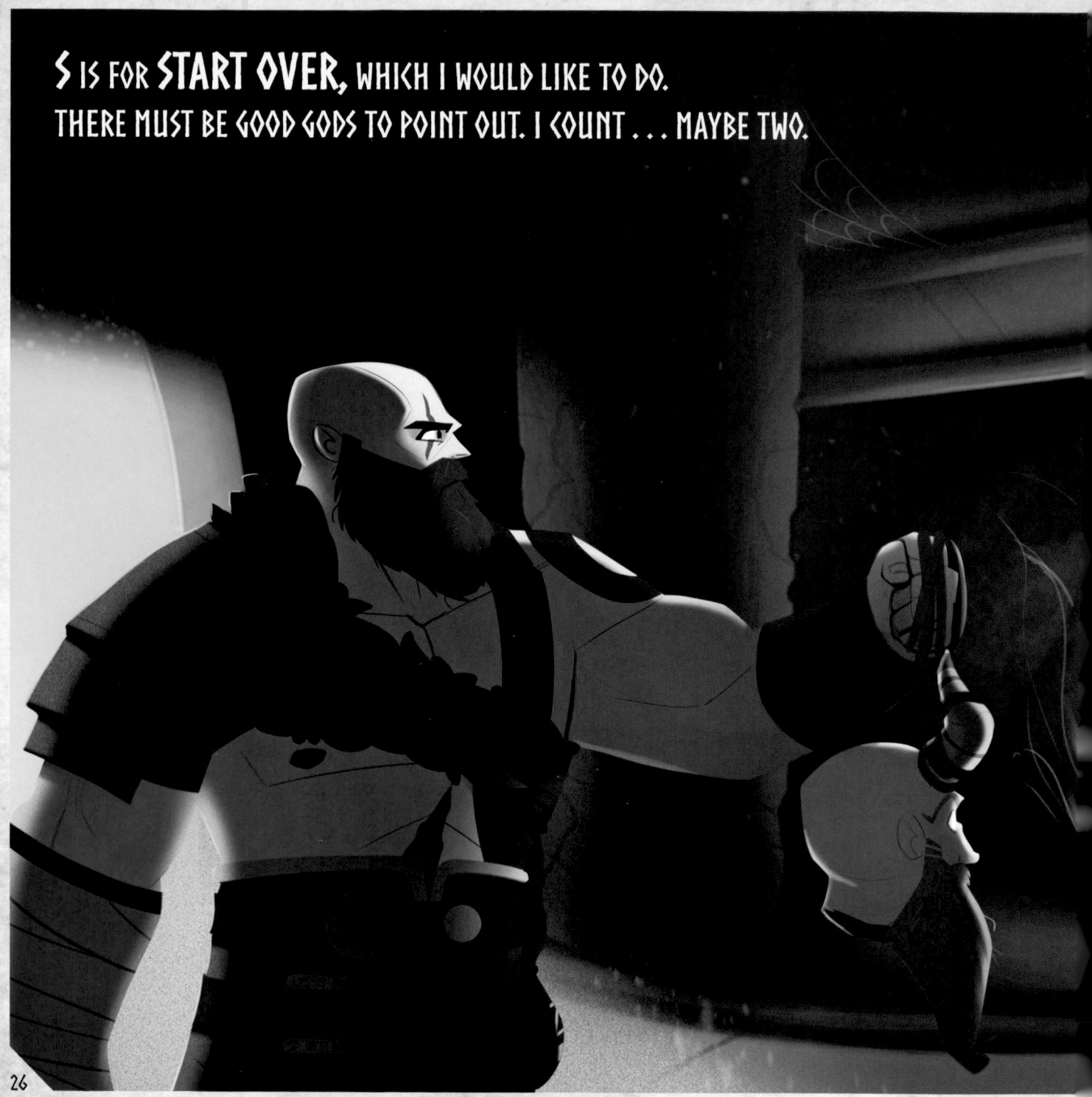
S IS FOR START OVER, WHICH I WOULD LIKE TO DO.
THERE MUST BE GOOD GODS TO POINT OUT. I COUNT . . . MAYBE TWO.

LIKE T IS FOR TÝR, GOD OF WAR WHO FOUGHT FOR PEACE.
U IS FOR UNDERSTAND? THIS BEHAVIOR MUST CEASE.
THAT SYMBOL. IT'S A BUNCH OF RUNES TOGETHER. PEACE. UNITY. HOPE.

FOR IF V IS FOR VENGEANCE, NOTHING IS DOWN THAT PATH BUT DOOM.
(WHEN ALL THIS IS OVER, I AM GOING TO LIE DOWN IN A DARK ROOM.)
I GUESS WE'RE THE BAD GUYS NOW.

**W** IS FOR **WHAT WOULD YOUR MOTHER SAY?** I WOULD LIKE TO KNOW.
WHAT DID SHE TEACH YOU? HOW DID SHE HELP YOU GROW?

**X** IS FOR **THAT BLANK SPACE SHE LEFT,** WITH NO ONE LEFT TO FILL,
AFTER WE TRUDGE TO THE TOP OF THIS GIANTS' HILL.

EXCEPT FOR **Y** IS FOR **YOU,** WHO MAKES ME BETTER—
AND HAS ON THIS JOURNEY WITH EVERY LETTER.
SO, YOUR DAD WAS **Z** FOR **ZEUS?** THAT'S CONVENIENT.

INSIGHT EDITIONS
PO BOX 3088
SAN RAFAEL, CA 94912
WWW.INSIGHTEDITIONS.COM

FIND US ON FACEBOOK: WWW.FACEBOOK.COM/INSIGHTEDITIONS
FOLLOW US ON TWITTER: @INSIGHTEDITIONS

Santa Monica Studio © 2020 SONY INTERACTIVE ENTERTAINMENT LLC. GOD OF WAR IS A TRADEMARK OF SONY INTERACTIVE ENTERTAINMENT LLC. ALL RIGHTS RESERVED.

ALL RIGHTS RESERVED. PUBLISHED BY INSIGHT EDITIONS, SAN RAFAEL, CALIFORNIA, IN 2020.

NO PART OF THIS BOOK MAY BE REPRODUCED IN ANY FORM WITHOUT WRITTEN PERMISSION FROM THE PUBLISHER.

LIBRARY OF CONGRESS CATALOGING-IN-PUBLICATION DATA AVAILABLE.

ISBN: 978-1-68383-889-0

PUBLISHER: RAOUL GOFF
PRESIDENT: KATE JEROME
ASSOCIATE PUBLISHER: VANESSA LOPEZ
CREATIVE DIRECTOR: CHRISSY KWASNIK
VP OF MANUFACTURING: ALIX NICHOLAEFF
DESIGNER: BROOKE MCCULLUM
EDITOR: AMANDA NG
EDITORIAL ASSISTANT: MAYA ALPERT
MANAGING EDITOR: LAUREN LEPERA
PRODUCTION EDITOR: JENNIFER BENTHAM
PRODUCTION MANAGER: EDEN ORLESKY

ROOTS of PEACE REPLANTED PAPER

INSIGHT EDITIONS, IN ASSOCIATION WITH ROOTS OF PEACE, WILL PLANT TWO TREES FOR EACH TREE USED IN THE MANUFACTURING OF THIS BOOK. ROOTS OF PEACE IS AN INTERNATIONALLY RENOWNED HUMANITARIAN ORGANIZATION DEDICATED TO ERADICATING LAND MINES WORLDWIDE AND CONVERTING WAR-TORN LANDS INTO PRODUCTIVE FARMS AND WILDLIFE HABITATS. ROOTS OF PEACE WILL PLANT TWO MILLION FRUIT AND NUT TREES IN AFGHANISTAN AND PROVIDE FARMERS THERE WITH THE SKILLS AND SUPPORT NECESSARY FOR SUSTAINABLE LAND USE.

MANUFACTURED IN CHINA BY INSIGHT EDITIONS

10 9 8 7 6 5 4 3 2